THE DOG ON THE LOG
WITH HIS FRIEND MR FROG

Written by Andrew Walker

With Illustrations by James Parkin & Kantarat Ulhaka

TINY TREE

*The Dog on the Log
with his Friend Mr Frog*
Published in 2025 by
Tiny Tree Books
West Wing Studios
Unit 166, The Mall
Luton, LU1 2TL
tinytreebooks.com

Copyright © 2025 Andrew Walker

The right of Andrew Walker to be identified as the author of this work has been asserted in accordance with the Copyright, Designs and Patents Act 1988.

All rights reserved. No reproduction, copy or transmission of this publication may be made without express prior written permission. No paragraph of this publication may be reproduced, copied or transmitted except with express prior written permission or in accordance with the provisions of the Copyright Act 1956 (as amended). Any person who commits any unauthorised act in relation to this publication may be liable to criminal prosecution and civil claims for damage.

All characters appearing in this work are fictitious.
Any resemblance to real persons, living
or dead, is purely coincidental.

To my children, you inspire me every day to get up and out of bed!

To all the silly dads out there - thank you for always being ready for an adventure, for never taking life too seriously and for sharing your love of laughter with your children. This book is dedicated to you and the memories we make together.

To anyone who has ever believed in me.

This is the story of a dog on a log
who lived quite happily in a smelly old bog.
This dog was scruffy, all covered in fleas
with a musty whiff and crazy knees.

His very best friend was Mr Frog,
who lived on a lily pad next to the log.

By contrast he was extremely clean,
collecting antiques which he liked to be seen.

The dog was clearly
not a sensible fellow,
He was sloppy and slobbish
and much too mellow.

He enjoyed making smells
with a pop, fizz or bam
and loved eating sausages
with baked beans and Spam.

One night the dog howled, which woke up his friend, he then let out a 'Parp!' which was hard to defend.

He'd foraged some food from some washed-up debris and guzzled down syrup, staying up until three!

The food Dog had eaten had been rather cheesy;
his stomach now rumbled and made him feel queasy.

"Excuse me old friend, I think you should know that my bottom feels odd and you really should go!"

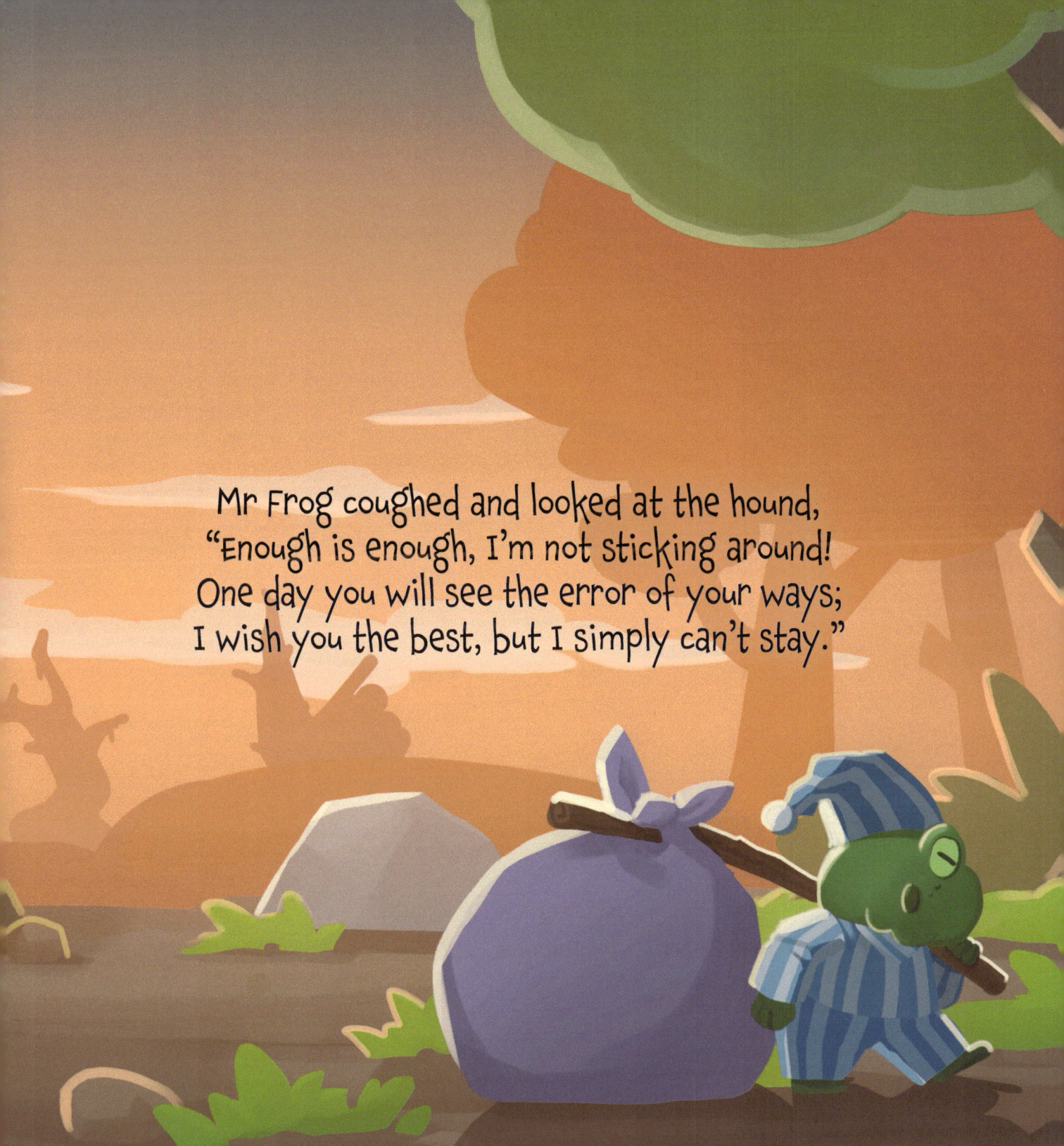

Mr Frog coughed and looked at the hound,
"Enough is enough, I'm not sticking around!
One day you will see the error of your ways;
I wish you the best, but I simply can't stay."

The golden sun soon began to set;
The dog was alone and felt full of regret.

He needed to learn to value his friends,
to sort himself out, and to make some amends.

Days turned to weeks but the Frog wasn't seen;

the dog tried to be cleaner, healthy and green.

The rains now set in and the clouds roared with thunder; the dog cowered down in the log he was under.

The thunder rolled on with a lighting whip-crack.
The dog missed his friend and wished he was back.
He peeped his head out, thought hard and then stood;
he howled, "I'm sorry!" as loud as he could.

"Hello my dear friend,
it's me, Mr Frog!
I want to come home;
I miss our old bog.
Let us forgive
and speak ill no more;
let us look to the future
and all that's in store."

Under the light of the moon the friends sat on the log, laughing and joking with some snacks from the dog.

Together they watched the fireflies dance,
feeling happy their friendship had a bright second chance.

A Lullaby

Scruffy dog, lying in bed,
with farts so loud they wake up the dead.
Mr Frog with a clever grin
says, "I know how to fix that din!"

Chorus:
Hush now, don't you cry;
Mr Frog will sing you a lullaby

Mr Frog croaks a melody,
Dog's farts turn into harmony;
making music together through the night
until everything feels just right.

Chorus:
Hush now, don't you cry;
Mr Frog will sing you a lullaby

Dog and frog, the best of friends,
sing their song until the end.
Tomorrow they'll play fetch and keep;
for now **sweet dreams** and **peaceful sleep**.